MOON RUNNER

MOON RUNNER

Carolyn Marsden

CANDLEWICK PRESS
CAMBRIDGE, MASSACHUSETTS

Copyright © 2005 by Carolyn Marsden

First paperback edition 2007

The Library of Congress has cataloged the hardcover edition as follows:

Marsden, Carolyn.

Moon runner / Carolyn Marsden. —1st ed.

p. cm.

Summary: When Mina discovers that she can run faster than her athletic friend, Ruth, she thinks she must choose between running and friendship.

ISBN 978-0-7636-2117-9 (hardcover)

[1. Friendship—Fiction. 2. Running—Fiction. 3. Racing—Fiction.] I. Title.

PZ7.M35135Mo 2005

[Fic]—dc22   2004058143

ISBN 978-0-7636-3304-2 (paperback)

2 4 6 8 10 9 7 5 3 1

Printed in the United States of America

This book was typeset in
Horley Old Style MT and Oxalis.

Candlewick Press
2067 Massachusetts Avenue
Cambridge, MA 02140

visit us at www.candlewick.com

For my beautiful moon runner,

Maleeka Vayna

 Chapter One

"Here." Mina handed Ruth the Friendship Ball.
"It's your turn now." The ball was made of bits
of multicolored yarn. Each day a different friend
took it home and added to it.

"The Friendship Ball is getting too huge,"
Ruth said, holding the yarn as if it were a bowling
ball, pretending to stagger. Her ponytail swung
back and forth.

"That's because we're all such good friends," Mina said. She stooped to pick up a bit of yarn that had come loose and floated to the sidewalk. They were walking in the feathery shade of the mesquite trees, toward the entry of the pink two-story building of Elizabeth Morris Elementary. A warm desert breeze stirred Mina's bangs. The March day would be hot.

"My soccer team took first place on Saturday." Ruth gave a thumbs-up. "We're the champs now."

"Cool," said Mina, though it seemed silly to care so much about chasing a soccer ball around a field.

"Today's the big day," Ruth said.

"What big day?"

"Don't you remember? Track. Coach said that all fourth and fifth graders would be starting this afternoon."

Oh, no, thought Mina. She must have forgotten on purpose. If kids goofed around whenever

Coach was giving instructions, they had to run laps. So Mina always stood at attention. She hated running. It was easier to put up with basketball. She could sort of pretend to play without doing much. Last year, at her old school, she hadn't had PE because the yard was too small.

They slipped into the courtyard just as the Pledge of Allegiance started. Mina put her hand over her heart and carefully said the pledge. When that was over, she sang the national anthem, almost hitting the high notes.

The other two Fellow Friends stood in front of her. Alana, who always wore black Mary Jane shoes with jeans shorts, turned around. "Here," she whispered, sprinkling candy powder from a packet into Mina's palm.

Mina sucked the sweet grains from her palm, and they turned to sugary, spicy syrup in her mouth.

Sammy, with his cowlick of blond hair, opened his cupped hands to show Mina a cricket.

"Let it go," she whispered.

Sammy opened his hands wider and the cricket leaped off.

They got into the line for Ms. Jenner's class. As the kids moved up the steps to the second floor, Mina wondered if she should pretend to be sick so she could miss track.

She noticed her reflection in the glass case full of school sports trophies: Mina Lee with straight black hair and narrow eyes. Mina Lee who cared nothing about sports or trophies.

When everyone was settled in the classroom, Ms. Jenner took attendance, then read the lunch menu: steak strips, French fries, green beans, and pudding.

Mina looked out the big window. The sky was a crisp blue, clear all the way to the horizon. The moon, almost invisible, still hung above the desert mountains. Without thinking, Mina sketched it in the margin of her notebook.

Ms. Jenner had all her students keep moon journals. She was nuts about the moon. Instead of a globe of the earth, she had one of the moon. She had a bookcase full of moon picture books, moon poetry, books of moon facts and moon myths. She had pictures of moon goddesses and of the first men to land on the moon.

Mina had done a report on the Chinese Moon Festival, which was held during the fall, when the moon was huge. Mom had come to school and helped everyone make round moon cakes with red bean paste inside.

It was time for silent reading. Mina took out her mystery, *Seven Steps to Treasure,* and began. The book was too easy for her. It had drawings at the beginning of each chapter. "Can't you read something more challenging?" Mom often said. Mom was a librarian, and reading was important to her. "You get cold feet when it comes to reading, Mina Lee." But Mina liked her mystery series.

The heroine had just found diamonds in the neighbor's yard. *The trunk was too heavy for Francesca to lift. So she looked around, then hid one diamond in her pocket.*

"And now, class," said Ms. Jenner, when the twenty minutes was up, "you have an hour to work on individual projects."

At the computer, Ruth and Mina traded the mouse back and forth as they clicked through one screen after another, looking for the website on tree frogs.

Once they got to the site, they oohed and aahed over the glowing creatures photographed in their jungle hideouts. They ran the mouse together, Ruth's hand on top of Mina's, scooting back and forth on the table.

Mina had started fourth grade here in the fall. She hadn't wanted to leave her tiny private school. She felt comfortable there and had had the same best friend since kindergarten. But the school only went through third grade. All summer Mina had worried about the plunge into the huge public school. Mostly she'd worried about making a new friend.

But it turned out that friends hadn't been a problem after all. The first day, a group of two girls and a boy had invited her to the shady picnic tables at lunchtime. Sammy wasn't like the other boys she'd known. He was never bossy, and he liked to talk about things the way girls did. By the end of the first week, Mina had traded phone numbers with Sammy, Alana, and Ruth.

In early October, Ruth had thrown a surprise party for Mina. The Fellow Friends had jumped out from behind the bushes wearing cone-shaped party hats. Ruth had read the official Fellow Friends certificates out loud: herself for being the athlete, Sammy for loving to collect bugs, Alana for being the best reader, and Mina for being the New Friend.

They taught her the Fellow Friends Handshake: *Shake with the right hand, patty-cake twice, snap, snap.*

Out on the patio, under the gigantic spreading black walnut tree, they sat down around a cake with *Fellow Friends Forever* on it. Because Mina was the guest of honor, Ruth handed her the knife. Mina had paused before slicing, not wanting to cut into the words linked together in cursive lines of frosting.

Afterward, because the weather was still hot, the Friends threw water balloons at each other and drank huge glasses of red punch.

PE was right after lunch. Coach Lombard waited in the middle of the field in his big, silly straw hat. As soon as everyone stood in formation, he named off the events: the high jump, the long jump, the softball throw, the quick sprint of the fifty meter, the exhausting five-hundred meter, the team relays . . . Mina noticed that as he talked, Ruth stretched her legs—first one, then the other—out in back of her, as though she couldn't wait to get started on all the events at once. But listening to Coach made Mina feel like lying down in the grass for a long nap.

"In two weeks, those of you who make the track team will be competing against the other schools in District 3 at Duncan Berring Elementary. Anyone who places first, second, or third at that meet will go on to the citywide meet. It's called City for short." Coach lifted his hat and smoothed his sweaty hair down with one hand.

Mina pushed at some pebbles with her toe.

"By the way," he added, "not all of you will practice all the events."

Well, that's one big relief, Mina thought.

Coach blew his whistle and gestured toward the field. "Laps first. But take your time. I don't want to see any showoff sprints. Pace yourselves so you can do at least three laps."

When Coach blew the whistle a second time, Ruth leaped forward as though no gravity held her down.

Mina took a deep breath, started running, and felt like a desert tortoise, storteling along with clunky, heavy limbs. Ahead, Ruth seemed to fly. How did she run so fast and easily? Mina had gone only half a lap, and breathing hurt. Maybe thinking about tortoises was a bad idea. There had to be a better animal. She imagined a roadrunner skipping along on tall, skinny legs.

To her surprise, she felt lighter right away. She passed under the mesquite tree, whose long branches provided five strides' worth of dark delicious shade. Her footsteps began to mark out a rhythm. She ran around the curve by the baseball diamond, toward the basketball courts. Why had she ever hated running? A lap wasn't so far, after all.

Roadrunner, roadrunner, she repeated to herself. The second time she crossed through the mesquite tree's shade, she was sailing. Her legs carried her effortlessly. She passed Alana chugging along with red cheeks. Ruth ran half a lap ahead, and Mina began to gain on her. A warm, dry breeze lifted the hairs around Mina's face as she ran. By the third lap, she remembered her favorite dream of flying off a snowy cliff and over a landscape speckled with pools of turquoise water. A half-moon hung like a promise in the daytime sky. In the dream, she'd glided, arms outstretched to hold the whole round Earth from one horizon to the other.

Chapter Two

"I did the coolest thing at school today," Mina told her little sister when Mom picked them up from school.

"Did you get Popsicles for snack?" asked Paige, pulling hard to open a bag of lemon drops, her black hair falling across her cheeks.

"Nope. I ran."

"Oooh, I love to run!" Paige handed Mina a candy.

Mom looked at them in her rearview mirror. "I hope that isn't something sweet I smell coming from the back seat."

Mina closed her mouth tight around the lemon drop. She and Paige exchanged smiles.

"I used to hate running," Mina said, shifting the candy to her cheek. "But today it felt fun."

"You'll probably win races," Paige said.

"I don't care about winning. That part doesn't matter."

"Take me running," Paige said.

"Mmm. Maybe." Mina pressed her forehead against the glass of the car window. When she imagined the run in her mind, she once again felt like a roadrunner racing along on tall, skinny legs, sometimes lifting into a low arc of flight. "Okay. Let's run super early tomorrow morning when the moon is still up."

As Mina and Paige approached the park near their house, a warm breeze swirled the fragrant smells of the springtime grass. The moon rested in the western sky, barely visible.

"We should stretch first," said Mina. "Hold on here." She guided Paige's hand to the fence, then showed her how to loosen her calf muscles.

Paige imitated Mina, then announced, "I feel all stretchy now."

"You don't look stretchy enough. Let's do windmills with our arms." Mina swung her arms backward, then forward, tracing giant circles.

They set out over the damp, spongy grass. Mina breathed in the freshness.

"Now faster," Paige demanded after they'd gone once around the field.

Mina quickened her stride, but not too much. Her little sister had to win this one.

"Look, Mina, we're racing the moon!" Paige shouted, pointing to the crescent that seemed to travel alongside them as they passed the monkey bars.

"Who'll win?" Mina asked.

"I will!" Paige declared and sprinted ahead. She rounded the curve and threw herself down, panting, at the spot where she and Mina had stretched.

"And you did win," said Mina, crash-landing beside Paige.

"Yup. The moon is in the same old place. And I even beat *you*, Mina."

They lay still together, the coolness seeping into their hot bodies. Mina stared up at the moon, so pale it almost looked transparent. She considered ways to record the morning run in her moon journal. "Don't forget to explore movement in your journals," Ms. Jenner had said. "Ancient peoples danced under the moon."

Mina hoped that running under the moon would count. A drawing of her and Paige? A poem? She hadn't raced *against* the moon, she thought, but rather she'd let the moon guide her. That wasn't a totally crazy idea. The moon's gravity pulled on the ocean, creating the tides. It pulled on all liquids. And she was ninety percent water.

Ms. Jenner had said to put music into the journals. Mina hummed a tune, making it up as she went along. Maybe she'd write a song about running with the moon: *The white moon carried me faster, lifting me like a wave in the sea.* . . .

Chapter Three

As they ran during PE that afternoon, Mina watched Ruth, who was half a lap ahead of her. Ruth's legs moved quickly while she kept the upper part of her body still. Her bent arms pumped back and forth.

Curious as to how it felt to move like that, Mina copied Ruth's style.

And again, she swirled into her flying dream with the earth rotating far below. Her feet hardly touched the grass, and her body grew tall. The air felt like a silk scarf slipping across her skin.

She began to overtake Ruth. That surprised her. People said that Ruth Largness was the fastest runner in the school, including the boys. Just as Mina was close enough to reach out and touch Ruth, Coach blew the whistle and beckoned everyone close.

Coach separated the boys from the girls. He had five high-school students working as helpers. "Line the kids up against the wall, tallest to shortest," he called out.

A girl named Addie, who wore a sweatshirt with *Girls Rule!* on it in glittery letters, took the girls to the wall by the cafeteria. "Stand back to back," she commanded. "I need to separate you into groups." Sometimes, she touched the tops of their heads with the flat of her hand, comparing heights. Finally, everyone got in order.

Coach gestured with his arm, making slicing movements: "Everyone on my right is in D group. You girls here are in C." And so on, until there were four groups.

Mina and Ruth were in class C, with those of medium height.

Alana, a little taller, ended up in class B.

"Why did coach divide us up like that?" Mina asked Ruth.

"To make it fair. Taller people with longer legs run faster."

The groups began to call names back and forth: "Shorties!"

"Beanpoles!"

"Shrimps!"

"Telephone poles!" Mina shouted along with Ruth.

A high-school kid with red hair took the boys to the high jump. The boy threw himself backward over a pole and landed on a big mattress.

"Look," Coach called out to another group. "I'm going to show you the long jump." He ran down the grass like an airplane getting ready to lift off. At the white line, he took a giant leap and landed in the sand. His floppy hat sailed off his head and fell onto the grass.

Mina and Alana giggled behind their hands.

Coach leaned down to pick up the hat. "Now, one by one, your group will try that."

He led the class C girls to the grass, which he'd marked off with spray chalk for fifty-meter sprints.

The first girl took off while Coach clocked her with his stopwatch. Then he wrote something down on his clipboard.

Mina wiggled a loose tooth with the tip of her index finger.

As they ran one by one, a fifth-grade girl with satiny running shorts asked Coach to show the times he'd written on the clipboard.

He laughed. "This information is just for me."

Mina was sure that Ruth would be the fastest. She not only had strong muscles, but she also liked to win.

Sammy stopped on the way back from the drinking fountain, wiping his mouth with the back of his hand. "Don't worry—you'll do fine. You've got those long, chopstick legs," he said to Mina. Together they watched Ruth at the starting line, deep into a lunge, ready to spring at the sound of Coach's whistle.

The whistle blew and Ruth darted forward, every bit of her focused on the white stripe painted on the grass. Coach pushed the button on his watch when her left foot touched the finish line.

Without thinking, Mina found herself bending into the same crouch as Ruth. At the whistle's shrill blast, she pushed off, the toes of her right foot digging deep into the grass. Her legs flashed beneath her. She lifted off the ground with each stride and shot toward the line, her muscles filled with fire. Only when she heard Coach's whistle again did she realize she had arrived.

✻   ✻   ✻

Waiting on Mina's bed when she got home was a surprise from Mom—a library book about tree frogs. Mina picked it up and flipped through it. There were a lot of words. She sat down with it, though, and looked at the photos.

"Like it?" Mom asked, coming into the room.

"A little," Mina admitted. "But it's kind of hard." In spite of herself, she began to read the captions under the photos. Not so hard after all. She concentrated and read more.

Her brain and eyes were working to travel across the pages, she thought, the same way her body had worked to cross the grass.

# Chapter Four

"A campout in my backyard would be so special," Alana said over the telephone that night.

"Maybe," Mina said slowly. She always made up excuses not to go on overnights. At home she knew what to expect.

Paige was watching a cartoon about three robots who kept getting into trouble. Poochie, Paige's chocolate-colored mutt, sat on the couch too, yipping at the exciting parts.

"Let me guess," Alana continued. "You're going out of town. You're getting a cold. How can you be so nervous about a stupid overnight? You're a track star now."

"A track star?" Mina asked.

One of the robots toppled down a hill. Poochie yipped.

"I know a secret about you. But I'll only tell it if you spend the night."

Mina shifted the phone to the other ear. A secret? What could Alana know?

"I think that's a yes I hear coming." Alana began to hum "For She's a Jolly Good Fellow."

Mina smiled. An overnight probably couldn't hurt. It might even be fun. "Okay. Yes, but I have to ask my mom."

"Yeah!" Alana shouted so loudly that Mina had to hold the phone away from her ear.

"I did not do my personal best," Alana said as she and Mina set out walking to her house. "I guess I'm too much of a girlie girl for sports."

Mina smiled. Ms. Jenner talked about personal best, especially when someone turned in a sloppy paper.

Alana held the Friendship Ball under one arm as she strolled.

They walked down the street lined with ornamental orange trees. Once Mina had tried to eat one of the beautiful fruits. It tasted bitter, but the blossoms still smelled like heaven. Mina stuck her nose into the white petals and sniffed.

"Watch out for bees," Alana said. "My dad got stung on the cheek once doing that."

At Alana's, they set up the tent in the backyard, then laid out the sleeping bags. The light coming through the yellow nylon made their faces glow.

Alana opened a bottle of nail polish and

Mina unzipped the tent flap to air out the strong smell.

Alana handed Mina the tiny brush, then held out her hands like two soft fans, the fingernails bitten off short.

Mina did fine until Alana's second pinkie. The polish smeared. She tried to rub it off with a tissue, but the polish rolled up in a wrinkly mess.

"That's okay. I'll fix it later," said Alana.

Mina spread her fingers. She was proud of her nails, grown out as long as Mom would allow. "Tell me the secret."

Alana coated Mina's thumbnail with red. "Well, I peeked at Coach's list."

"And?"

"You really want to know?" Alana moved on to the pointer finger.

Mina hesitated.

"It's an important secret," Alana insisted.

"Well, tell me, then."

"When Coach wrote down the times, I saw your time and Ruth's." Alana took a big breath. "You beat her."

Mina waited for Alana to break out laughing and say, *Just kidding!*

But Alana wasn't even smiling. She dipped the brush in the bottle and lifted it out, loaded with polish.

The inside of the tent bloomed with the smell of Fire Truck Red.

"How could you see what Coach wrote?" Mina asked. "He wrote too small. He hid the page."

"Nuh-uh. I stood on the bench behind him and saw real good. Ruth's gonna be surprised. She thinks you're a girlie girl like me. She's gonna have a fit."

Ruth have a fit? Mina didn't want that. She enjoyed soaring along like a bird caught on a current of air—but she didn't care about winning. Ruth cared. Ruth had always won, and she should keep on winning. If Ruth had a fit, it might hurt their friendship. The Fellow Friends might become Non-Fellow Enemies.

Alana moved quickly from nail to nail. When she finished, she leaned over and blew on the wet polish. "Now our hands look extra pretty for cat's cradle. Hold up your fingers," she commanded, pulling a string from her pocket. "Don't worry—the polish is dry." She placed the string over Mina's extended fingers, threading the outlines of the Walking Turtle.

For dinner, Mina and Alana drank Italian cream sodas flavored with raspberry and ate pineapple pizza, throwing the crusts to the birds. When it got dark, they lay back in their sleeping bags and listened to the crickets rasping their legs together in the bushes.

Just before she fell asleep, Mina felt a little homesick. To distract herself, she ran the fifty-meter sprint again in her mind, crossing the grass as though lifted by the breeze, the warm sunshine pouring through her.

Mina opened her eyes to yellow light playing across the walls of the tent and felt another sting of homesickness for her own bed, for Mom, Daddy, and Paige.

She unzipped her bag, crawled to the tent door, and scanned the sky. At first she didn't see the moon because the sky was light blue, the sun up. Her yellow pencil wouldn't be half bright enough for that blazing sun.

"I don't think we have to draw it on weekends," said Alana behind her, still in her sleeping bag.

But Mina was already reaching under her pillow for her moon journal. Drawing the moon was familiar.

As she sketched, she thought of how Ms.

Jenner said ancient people believed Moon Trees grew on the moon. The gods flew to the moon to harvest the fruit and make a drink from the juice. The magical drink made them wise, happy, and allowed them to live forever.

Finishing her drawing, Mina wondered if the Moon Trees smelled like the soft, sweet puffs of orange blossom drifting into Alana's backyard.

She imagined herself running lightly around a Moon Tree, launching herself into great leaps through the sweetness.

Alana rolled the Friendship Ball to the center of the tent. The art teacher had given her scraps of yarn left over from a weaving project.

Mina went back inside and the two of them worked, untangling and winding, making sure that the ball was round on all sides.

"It's almost summer. We'll have a bunch of pool parties and overnights," Alana declared. "Even Sammy. He can have his own tent."

"That all sounds fun," Mina said. She held

the Friendship Ball in her lap, the weight comforting her. As Alana talked, Mina felt her whole world grow wider. She stretched out her legs and sighed.

"Ruth's out of town for her soccer match," Alana said. "I wonder how it's going."

Ruth. Mina had beaten her. Alana had seen the proof. Mina tucked her legs back in. A gust of wind came up, blowing the branches of the tree across the sun, casting a shadow over the yellow tent.

Chapter Five

At school on Monday, Mina and Ruth set to work on the frog project. First they colored the big piece of cardboard with shades of green so that it looked like the rain forest. While Ruth cut out the pictures of the tree frogs they'd downloaded from the website, Mina copied her notes in her neatest penmanship. *When tree frogs get cold, they hide in the mud.*

Mom told her she got cold feet. And sometimes Mom called her a stick-in-the-mud. *I like to hide in the mud like a cold tree frog,* Mina thought.

She worked hard to concentrate on her lettering. *Don't get cold feet now,* she instructed herself. She worried that her hand might slip and spoil a letter. What would Ruth think?

While Mina worried, Ruth sang a little song under her breath. "You're in my life forever, ta-da-da, forever . . ."

Mina put down her pen and looked at Ruth. Would she be singing that happy song, just loud enough for Mina to hear, if she knew Mina had beaten her in the fifty meter?

In the afternoon, storm clouds let loose with a quick little rain. By the time PE started, the sky sparkled with light. The dark clouds made the new leaves look extra green, the stucco walls of the school pinker. Stepping onto the wet grass, Mina found herself looking forward to running.

Then a cloud covered the sun and she shivered.

The cloud moved and the sun shone. The arc of a rainbow appeared. Mina stretched, raising both arms high into the freshly washed air.

Once again, Coach sent the boys off with the high-school helpers and grouped the girls according to height.

The class C girls lined up. Coach wouldn't time them today. They'd all run together. Mina didn't want to stand next to Ruth, but Ruth came over to her. "Just think *finish line,*" she advised.

When Coach blew the whistle, Mina jetted forward. She dashed over the wet grass, the clouds overhead, the rainbow shining, each precious instant pushing her onward: *one-two-three-four-five-six* . . .

At the last second, Mina sensed Ruth next to

her and turned to look. The look slowed her just the teeniest bit. When she arrived at the white stripe, Coach shouted, "Tie!" He held up Mina's arm and Ruth's.

Ruth stared at Mina, her mouth open as she panted for breath.

Mina had once heard a strange word: *unquiet*. It meant more than "not quiet." It meant deeply uneasy. She was unquiet now, with Ruth staring at her, looking as though she'd come home to find her house flattened by a dust devil.

Coach dropped their arms and patted Mina on the back. "Congratulations. Don't look so surprised, Mina."

Ruth held out her hand. "Congratulations." But she didn't look Mina in the eye.

Mina thought that the handshake was probably something sportswoman-like that Ruth had learned in soccer.

When the class B girls ran the fifty meter,

Alana came in third to last, jogging in her black Mary Janes. She threw up her hands and laughed. Sammy caught up with Mina on the way back to the classroom. "I saw you race. Way to go!" He held out his hand, waiting for the Fellow Friends Handshake.

Mina shook his hand, slapped his palms twice, then snapped her fingers twice. But she also glanced ahead, to where Ruth walked across the lunch patio. She hoped that Ruth was too far away to hear Sammy's congratulations. The rainbow had dissolved into the blue sky.

During silent reading, Mina only pretended to read. Even though the owner of the diamonds was following Francesca, Mina just stared at her book. Mom was right. It was a baby book.

She put one hand on each knee, bony and round under her jeans. Her legs seemed like the legs of a stranger, legs that had run all on their own.

But they *weren't* the legs of a stranger, she thought. They were her legs, and because of her they had run fast. As fast as the fastest girl. A tingle rose along her spine.

Although Ruth faced away from Mina, Mina could see that she wasn't turning the pages of her book either.

Chapter Six

Ms. Jenner had given everyone a sheet of water-color paper and a box of watercolors to take home. Mina spread out the paper, paints, and some crayons on the picnic table in the backyard.

The moon was a slice so thin that she had to sharpen the crayon to a fine point. The white shavings fell like shavings of the moon itself.

Mina poured watery paint onto the paper and let it run, saturating the fibers.

"That's so pretty," said Paige, sitting down next to Mina on the bench.

Mina edged her elbow out protectively. "Careful not to touch it while it's wet."

"Mommy says there's a rabbit on the moon."

"That's just what Chinese people pretend they see," Mina explained.

"Just pretend? It's not really there?"

Mina laughed. "No rabbit, Paige. It's craters and moon mountains that *look* like a rabbit."

"Oh, wow!" Paige leaned over Mina's elbow and pointed. "The paint doesn't stick to the moon you colored with crayon. It's still white!" She tilted her head back and scanned the sky. "I don't see the moon, Mina."

"It's not there now. I memorized the way it looked this morning."

"You got a good memory, Mina," Paige commented, then turned quickly on the bench.

"Daddy's home!" She ran to Daddy's truck as it pulled into the driveway.

"I've got a mealworm called Charlie," Paige told Daddy as he opened the truck door and stepped out, "and Mina won."

"What's a mealworm?" he asked.

"It's brown and this long." Paige held her fingers apart. "I have to feed it cut-up apples. And soon it's going to come home."

Daddy faked a shudder. "And Mina won what? A trip to Hawaii? A chocolate cake?"

"No, silly. She tied for first place in a running contest!" Paige skipped in a circle.

Mina closed her box of watercolors and waved to Daddy.

"Hey, what's this I hear?" he called.

"I did pretty good at running the fifty meter."

"Let's see how good." Daddy reached back into the truck for his measuring tape. He began to mark off fifty meters on the long driveway.

Mina double knotted her sneakers, then laid sticks down for the start and finish lines.

Daddy pushed buttons on his watch so that, instead of the time, the face displayed all zeros.

What kind of time would the watch show? Mina didn't know what her time had been when she'd tied Ruth.

She leaned over the starting line as Ruth had done.

"One, two, three—go!" shouted Paige, and Mina took off, Poochie running beside her, yipping, her floppy ears flapping. Run, run, run, run, run, and Mina crossed the finish line!

Paige checked the numbers and called out the time: 7.9 seconds.

Mina ran again, and her time was better: 7.3 seconds. She ran again, and her time was worse.

Daddy gave her a hug when she panted and wobbled after the third run. "Pretty soon you won't be wearing flowers anymore." He tugged at her purple shirt. "Just stripes or some other sporty design. Take a look at that." He pointed to her calf.

Mina flexed her foot and the muscle stood out along her bare lower leg. She was sure it hadn't been like that before. She flexed her other foot. The same.

"You're like Wonder Woman, Mina," said Paige. "Or, I know!" She ran to the picnic table and picked up Mina's painting. "You're a Moon Runner!"

Poochie yipped. Mina and Daddy laughed. "Great name," Daddy said.

Mina reached down and touched the muscles. They were firm under her hand. She stood up and put her hands on her hips. She smiled to herself. *Moon Runner.* She liked the sound.

 Chapter Seven

"We're missing recess," Mina complained. She and Alana were waiting for Sammy and Ruth by the hall door. "I don't think they stayed back with Ms. Jenner," Alana said, peering into the dark hallway. "Not unless they had to," Mina said. Then: "Look!" She'd spotted the two of them running across the playground. "They must have gone out the other door."

"Creeps," said Alana, but she waved at Sammy as he looked in their direction.

Sammy waved back. He said something to Ruth, but she didn't slow down or turn around.

"That's okay," Alana said. "I brought string for cat's cradle."

Mina watched Ruth and Sammy go to the far corner of the grass. Holding on to the chainlink fence, they walked along the narrow ledge separating the playground from the street, playing at being tightrope walkers.

It wasn't Mina's imagination. Ruth was avoiding her.

Alana had brought out the string. "Come on — let's sit down."

Mina held up her hands and let Alana do the tricks.

"Hold your fingers straight," Alana commanded.

Mina peeked at Ruth and Sammy again.

Alana arranged Mina's fingers one by one. "What's wrong with you today?"

Mina forced herself to pay attention to Alana's game of baby-in-the-cradle. If she didn't cooperate, Alana might go play with Sammy and Ruth, on the ledge, leaving her alone.

Ruth had abandoned her, and there had been no moon in the sky that morning, *This is the dark phase,* Mina thought.

Along the fence, where the mower hadn't reached, grew the purple flowers of alfilaria. Mina bent down to pick two long seedpods. "I'm not sure the Fellow Friends will last the year," she said, threading the seedpods together.

"Why not?" Alana asked.

"Ruth doesn't like me anymore. See how she's only playing with Sammy?"

"The Fellow Friends breaking up would be too sad." Alana poked out her lower lip. "I wish you and Ruth would be nice to each other."

"Maybe I'll just be friends with you," Mina said quickly. With her fingernail, she poked a hole in one seedpod. She threaded the other seedpod through the hole, making a pair of scissors.

"That wouldn't be the same," Alana answered.

"I know." Mina chopped at the air with her tiny green shears.

The whistle blew for the fifty-meter tryouts, and the class C girls took off.

Mina could hear the swish of Ruth's nylon running shorts and could smell her lemony shampoo. Suddenly she thought of Sammy and Ruth playing on the ledge without her. Of the way the Fellow Friends were falling apart. Of Alana's disappointment. Instead of trying hard, her body eased, like a rubber band that stretches and then relaxes. She fell back.

"Ruth Largness first! Shawndra Lopez second! Liz Barret third! Cassie Corbis fourth!" Coach shouted as they each came in.

Mina didn't count how many other girls finished ahead of her. She could have done better. Maybe not well enough to beat Ruth, but at least well enough to place in the top four.

The breath caught in her throat like a drink of water that had gone down the wrong way.

In the afternoon, Mina and Ruth worked on the frog project. Instead of sitting next to Mina, Ruth took the photos to organize at a table across the room.

Mina copied onto the poster board: *The red-eyed tree frog changes its color when it changes its mood. It can be dark green or a reddish brown.*

Ruth changed like a tree frog, too, she thought. When Mina had been only a girlie girl, Ruth had been friendly. But now that Mina competed with her, Ruth ignored her. She felt like saying *I lost the race on purpose.* Just the thought made her bite the inside of her cheek. Why was Ruth still acting so cold?

Mina replayed the tryouts in her mind. She'd thought she didn't care about winning, but losing had felt terrible.

At the end of science period, Ms. Jenner rang a chime.

Mina held the baggie open for the photos, and Ruth slid them in without touching Mina's fingers.

As the class sat in a circle on the rug, Ms. Jenner passed around a picture of an ancient moon goddess. "The ancient Greeks called her Hecate," she said.

"Why does she have three heads?" Sammy asked.

"Can anyone guess?"

"Like, 'cause the moon looks three different ways?" suggested Clarisa, who sat next to Mina in the circle.

"Yes, and because of the three phases, the ancient peoples thought the moon had three different personalities," Ms. Jenner continued. "Some thought the crescent moon looked like a knife. The full moon seems to bring blessings. People believed that in her dark phase, the moon makes people go crazy."

Sammy caught Alana's attention, then traced circles in the air with his index finger.

Alana stuck her tongue out at him.

The moon changed the way the red-eyed tree frogs did. The way Ruth did.

Mina thought about her own different faces. She wanted to win. She wanted to lose. She wanted to beat her friend. She wanted to keep her friend. Sometimes she just didn't know what she wanted, who she was. There was the old stick-in-the-mud self and the new Moon Runner self and someone in between. She felt as three-faced as the moon.

Chapter Eight

At a special meeting after school, Coach sat everyone down at the lunch tables. It was time to announce the teams that would compete at Duncan Berring Elementary. First he announced the boys, reading from the paper on his clipboard. The boys popped up and down and cheered when their names were read. Sammy didn't make a team. But then again, he'd told Coach a long time ago that he'd be visiting his grandparents the weekend of the meet.

Coach announced the girls' class D team, pausing between announcements for the noise to die away.

Mina straightened the fabric of her shorts, matching the stripes so they ran evenly from one side to the other. After her miserable finish in the fifty meter, she was sure she wouldn't be on the Elizabeth Morris Elementary team.

"And on the class C fifty-meter relay team: Ruth, Shawndra, Liz, and Cassie."

All four girls stood up and shouted, "Yes!" and slapped one another's palms.

Mina sucked in a breath of air. But she'd been right. Even though she could run fast, she wouldn't be competing. She wasn't a racer after all. Mina closed her eyes and pressed her fingertips to her eyelids to keep from crying.

She heard Coach take in a breath, preparing for the next announcement: "And on the class C fifty-meter sprint: Mina Lee and Ruth Largness."

Mina opened her eyes. At first a little flame of excitement rose up in her—she'd made it! Had she heard right? Ruth had stood up and was looking at her. Mina stood too and then Ruth sat down. No palm slapping. No Fellow Friends Handshake.

Mina focused on the asphalt underneath the picnic table. She scraped at the loose bits with her toe. Two Fellow Friends competing against each other.

She glanced in Ruth's direction. How did Ruth feel? Did she think Coach's assignment was a joke? Or was she a little worried?

But Ruth didn't seem to be thinking about Mina.

She and the other three relay racers huddled together in a clump. They whispered some lovely secret, then burst apart with a cheer.

I ought to be excited, too, Mina thought. She'd

made the team, after all. She'd made it without even being an athlete.

Yet instead of running with friends, she'd be running alone, against a friend. Sure, she'd be running against the girls from the other schools, but especially against Ruth. Only one girl would win first place.

"I'm in the fifty-meter sprint," Mina told Mom as Mom fixed celery and peanut butter for Paige.

"My goodness, what big news," Mom said. "Such a surprise, Mina."

Mina ran her fingertip along the sharp edge of the countertop. She wished the news was as good as Mom thought.

Mom continued: "I want to see this with my own eyes, honey. Let's go practice at the park. I haven't jogged in weeks. I could use a run."

Mom handed the celery sticks to Paige. "Bring these along, sweetie."

The park lawn had just been mowed, the marks of the tractor mower imprinted in the soft, flattened grass. A eucalyptus tree cast dark green shadows.

Paige dashed to the swings and pumped her way up.

"Fly high, little hummingbird!" Mom shouted at Paige.

Mom jogged in place, then moved onto the grass. "I feel like I have two sacks of potatoes tied to my hips!" she shouted.

Mina had to laugh. She began to sprint, passing Mom.

"Go slow," Mom said.

But Mom's jogging looked like a funny walk. Mina wanted to show off. She wanted Mom and Paige to see her as the champion that she was. She went once around the edge of the park as fast as she could. Then she got a cramp in her side. She bent over and pressed on her ribs, but the pain didn't go away.

Mina sat down on a bench and observed Mom's slow progress—twice around, three times, four times.

Paige pumped the swing as high as it could go, the chains creaking against the horizontal pole.

Mom just kept plugging along. At least Mom was still running while Mina sat, a champ with a cramp.

Finally, Mom stopped and joined Mina on the bench. She rested her forearms on her thighs, her hands clasped together, and caught her breath.

"There's more I haven't told you," Mina said suddenly. She put her feet side by side so that the toes of her sneakers lined up exactly. She hadn't planned to talk about the painful stuff.

"About the team?"

Mina squeezed her feet tightly together. "I didn't get chosen for the relay team. Ruth's on it, but not me."

"Well, at least you made a team. That's a big deal."

Mina sighed. Could Mom understand? "But I'm running against Ruth in the fifty meter. She's on the individual, like me. If I win, our Fellow Friends group will fall apart for sure." Her voice grew high and thin. "If I let Ruth win, I'll feel icky about myself."

"I'm beginning to see." Mom straightened up and stretched her arms across the back of the bench.

"Something important happened the other day: Ruth has always been the fastest girl, but I tied her."

"That's quite something, Mina. Maybe Coach put you and Ruth both on the individual to break the tie."

"Maybe." Mina considered Mom's idea. "And there's something else." She told Mom about the running times Alana had seen on Coach's clipboard.

Mom whistled. After a moment, she stood

up and took Mina's hand, lifting her from the bench.

The two set off across the grass. Mina jogged as slowly as Mom did. Her feet touched the grass with soft, even thuds. Gradually, she forgot about Coach and his choice, Ruth and the team, and winning and losing.

Her breathing took on a rhythm—*easy, easy, slow, slow, slow.* She became aware of all the different parts of her feet—the little bones, the padded area of the sole, the round heels. Her footsteps landed, *now and now and now.* The earth turned up to meet her steps.

Chapter Nine

At lunchtime the next day, Mina found Coach at the last table on the end. "Could I talk to you?" she asked.

He nodded and gestured to the spot in front of him.

Mina sat down and set her paper lunch bag in her lap. She began to roll and unroll the top fold.

Coach laid his sandwich on its plastic baggie while he unscrewed the top of his thermos. He poured purple juice into a cup.

Mina thought about taking out her sandwich and munching away while she chatted with Coach. But she wanted to focus completely on what she had to ask. She plunged ahead: "I'm in the individual fifty meter and I've never run in a track meet before."

Coach took a bite of his cheese on whole wheat.

"I'm kind of nervous. I was wondering if I could trade with someone and run with my friend Ruth Largness on the relay team instead." The top fold of her lunch bag was becoming as soft as an old baby blanket.

Coach swallowed and swigged his juice. "Is that the real reason, Mina?"

Mina looked around. Ruth and Sammy sat at a far table. She didn't see Alana, who was probably looking for her. A quick glance toward the basketball court took in Cassie from the relay team, walking with friends.

Did she dare tell the truth out loud?

Coach squinted at her in the bright sunlight, as though to see her better, as though urging her to trust him.

"I'm afraid of beating Ruth. She might not be friends with me if I do."

Coach laughed. "That's not how most athletes would look at it. But go on."

"I'd feel better running *with* Ruth, on the relay team, instead of against her in the individual."

"If you beat Ruth, she can take it. She may get miffed, but she won't fall apart."

"But I don't want to hurt my friend."

"Mina," Coach said gently, swirling the juice around and around in the cup, "there's a lot of responsibility in running on a team. I kept you off the relay team because of your inexperience. A lot's at stake for your teammates. Worse than running against Ruth and beating her in the individual would be to run the relay and lose the race for Ruth and the other girls. Are you prepared to take that risk?"

So Mom had been wrong. Coach hadn't meant to set her up against Ruth. He was only protecting the team. Mina sat up straighter. "I know I'm new to sports, but I do run fast. I don't think I'd let the team down."

Coach finished his sandwich, balled up the baggie, and put it into his lunch box. He drained the last of the juice, leaving a line of purple above his upper lip.

"I don't usually make changes once I've made up my mind." He paused and looked at Mina.

It seemed as though he wasn't really looking at her, but at imaginary possibilities, picturing the races and all the different outcomes, good and bad. Mina clutched the top of her lunch bag.

"I'll tell you what, Mina. I won't do the

changing. It'll be up to you to convince one of those girls to change with you. You have my permission to ask them."

Mina let go of her lunch bag and stretched out her fingers.

After Coach had packed up and left, Mina found Cassie on the playground, near the basketball hoops. She was trading a cookie for a juice box.

"Can I ask you something, Cassie?" Mina still held her bag of uneaten lunch. "In private?"

Cassie got up from her friends and walked across the basketball court with Mina.

Mina deliberately walked on one of the white stripes—as though the straightness could guide her words. "I was wondering if you'd trade places with me. Run my fifty meter and let me run on the relay team."

"Why?" Cassie asked.

"Because Ruth Largness is my good friend and I'd like to run with her."

Cassie stared into the sky above the basketball hoops. "No, I can't do it. My softball throw is happening at the same time as the individual fifty meter. Sorry."

"Thanks anyway," said Mina. She walked off the straight white line and onto the wide expanse of grass.

During library time right after lunch, Mina whispered to Liz behind the shelves of biographies.

Liz didn't even ask why Mina wanted to change. She just said loudly, making no attempt to whisper: "The fifty meter is over with too quickly." Liz snapped her fingers. "Just like that. Even though I won't be running the whole time, the relay lasts four times as long. Just think, though—if you win the individual, you get all the glory."

Mina knelt down to tie her shoes.

✳   ✳   ✳

Mina caught up with Shawndra on the way to PE. When Mina asked the favor, Shawndra shrugged. "Doesn't make any difference to me."

"Let's tell Coach now, then," said Mina. She didn't want Shawndra to change her mind.

They waited until Coach Lombard had finished assigning his high-school helpers for the day. He fanned himself with his big hat as he talked.

When Coach turned to Mina and Shawndra, Mina was afraid he might have forgotten their lunchtime conversation.

"Shawndra's trading with me. Remember we talked about that?" Mina shifted from one foot to the other.

Coach continued to fan himself. "Are you sure about this, Mina?"

"Yes, Coach Lombard." She nodded in case he hadn't heard her.

But as she was walking away, a new thought struck her. Maybe Ruth wouldn't want her on the team. Maybe she'd been happy with the way things were. Maybe she planned to make Cassie, Liz, and Shawndra her new Fellow Friends.

At home, on her bed, Mina found another library book that Mom had left her. On the cover was a woman running. Mina picked the book up. Inside, there were a few photos and miles of tiny words.

At first her brain marched slowly over the words, but then it began to jog, and then to run as Mina grew interested in the story of Wilma Rudolph, who had overcome polio and wearing an ugly leg brace and teasing by other kids to become the world's fastest woman runner.

As Mina read, all of her own problems seemed like such little stuff. Even losing a friendship was nothing compared with almost not being able to walk, much less run.

 Chapter Ten

The next afternoon, the relay team had the first practice. The sun flooded the playground with a yellow, even heat. Flutters of hot air rose from the flagstones of the lunch patio.

Mina faced the girls with her hands in her pockets and announced: "Coach traded me with Shawndra."

No one said a thing. Ruth began to fiddle with the rubber band on her ponytail.

Coach strode over from the long jump. "We don't have a real track here, so we'll have to pretend. Each of you will stand fifty meters apart around a big oval. I've marked your places."

An orange cone stood behind Coach. Mina shaded her eyes with her hand and looked off at the other three cones. "Cassie," Coach continued, "you're the first runner and will start here. Then Liz." He pointed to the cone near the basketball court. "Mina."

Mina's cone rested under the shade of the mesquite tree.

"And Ruth, you're by the fence."

When Coach handed Cassie the baton, Mina leaned over to check out the slim, metal stick.

"Now, Cassie, when I blow my whistle, you're going to shoot off like a rocket and take that baton to Liz. Liz will buzz along and hand it to Mina. Mina will blast off to Ruth, the final runner."

They practiced the race four times, circling

the grass. Each time, Mina put the baton firmly in Ruth's outstretched hand.

At the end, when Coach said, "The team's time is very good," Mina noticed that he smiled especially at her.

Ruth went to pick up something she'd hidden under her sweatshirt. It was the Friendship Ball. "Here." She handled the ball as though it were a bundle of dirty laundry, handed it over to Mina while yelling to Cassie, "Hey, wait for me!"

Mina lay back into her pillow and ruffled the pages of *Seven Steps to Treasure*. Francesca had been kidnapped by the owner of the diamonds but had found her way out of the dark basement by following a string she'd cleverly dropped behind her as she went.

String. Suddenly, Mina remembered the Friendship Ball.

She jumped up and rushed into the living

room, where her backpack rested on the couch. No Friendship Ball.

She'd left it in the art room after the bell rang. She could see it clearly, sitting on the side counter.

What if the janitor threw it away? The ball looked kind of ratty.

Or what if another kid took it? Kids from all over the school were curious about the Friendship Ball and wanted to know what was so special about it. Some even joked that there was treasure hidden inside.

Mina looked at her watch: 8:02. The school building was closed.

She drank hot milk with cinnamon and counted bighorn sheep, but she couldn't sleep.

She imagined the Friendship Ball rolling down the hallway and into the street. As it rolled, it came undone, the scraps of yarn flying off in the wind until it was nothing but the core of itself—a tiny knot of red yarn that untied and blew away.

Mina leaned up on her elbow and opened the window. The cool night air burst into the room. How would the Fellow Friends feel if she'd lost the ball? They'd worked on it together all year, adding to it as their friendship grew. Even though she was the new Friend, they'd trusted her with the precious Friendship Ball. And now . . . Mina lay back down, pulled the blanket over her head, and nestled deep.

Mina banged on the doors of the school early the next morning. Someone had to be inside, because the lights were on in the southern wing.

Finally, Mr. Clark came, his ring of keys bouncing at his hip. "The before-school program isn't open yet," he announced, pushing the door open a crack.

"Please let me in for just a sec," said Mina. "I left something important in the art room. It's an emergency."

Mr. Clark shrugged. "I'll let you look up there. But then you'll have to wait on the playground."

She followed him up the stairs in the gloom of early dawn.

At the door to the art room, Mr. Clark paused while he sorted through the bunch of keys.

Mina tried to peek through the frosted glass.

The door opened, and right away, Mina saw that the counter was empty. Down on her hands and knees, she searched under the tables, opened the shelves, letting the doors clatter. *It has to be here. It has to be.* She searched each spot again.

Finally, she lifted both hands to Mr. Clark. "It's not here."

Mr. Clark grunted and motioned Mina toward the door.

During morning recess, Sammy found some ladybugs over by the fence. Crawling on hands and knees, he, Alana, and Ruth began to hunt them in the long grass.

Mina hung back. How could she confess to everyone that she'd lost the Friendship Ball?

"Look," Ruth was saying, "I got this from the garbage can." She held up a juice carton. "It can be a ladybug house."

Mina walked five steps until she stood over them. "Friends," she began.

Alana and Sammy looked up.

"Friends. I've done something awful."

Sammy sat up and rocked back onto his heels.

Alana shaded her eyes with her hand.

Ruth pulled the long blades of the grass apart, still searching for ladybugs.

Mina took a big breath. "I lost the Friendship Ball."

There was a silence, then Sammy said, "You're kidding. Where?"

"If she knew, it wouldn't be lost," Alana said.

Ruth said nothing.

Sammy concentrated on a ladybug creeping across his freckled hand. "It's okay, Mina. It was just stupid yarn."

"Yeah," said Alana.

Ruth yanked up a clump of grass. Dirt dangled from the roots. "Are you guys crazy? It wasn't just the stupid yarn but all our friendship wound up in there." She threw the grass in Mina's direction. "You were never a real Fellow Friend if you weren't careful of our ball and went and lost it."

Mina stepped back. Ruth was so wrong. She *had* been careful. She'd worried all night and had gotten to school super early to search and search the art room. . . .

"That was mean, Ruth," said Alana, jumping up. "Don't cry, Mina. We'll find the ball."

Mina was standing in the lunch line when she heard: "Close your eyes and turn around."

Sammy put something round into her arms.

Mina held the soft moon of the Friendship Ball close. "Oh!" was all she could say. She pressed her face against the yarn, smelling its mustiness, the scent of good memories wound into the roundness. Her whole body relaxed.

"Get out of line." Sammy touched Mina's forearm. "You don't want cafeteria food. You can eat some of my lunch."

"I promise never to lose it again," she said as they crossed the lunch patio, heading toward the picnic tables. "Double promise. I swear."

"I know you weren't careless. Don't worry."

"Where did you find it?"

"During math, I passed a note offering a twenty-five-cent reward. A kid gave it to me as we were lining up for lunch."

"That was so lucky, Sammy."

They sat down and Sammy handed over half an egg salad sandwich.

Mina ate with the Friendship Ball on her lap, one arm curved around it. "Ruth is probably still going to be mad."

"Probably." Sammy opened a bottle of pink lemonade. He held it out to her.

Mina took a sip. "She's mad about stuff other than the Friendship Ball."

"Yeah, it's kind of hard for her to be Athlete of the School and then maybe not be."

"So you know about that? She told you?"

"Not told me. But it's pretty obvious."

Mina finished the sandwich and Sammy offered her a carrot stick.

"One of you's gotta start solving things, though," Sammy said. "Otherwise you and her won't be friends. And if that happens, our group will bust up."

"I'm supposed to go to her house tomorrow to practice our science presentation."

"A perfect chance to talk."

"But Sammy"—Mina handed back the pink lemonade—"I'm afraid to bring it up."

"Pretend you're in a race. Pretend that you can't hang back but have to be strong and go forward." Sammy drained the lemonade, then played with the clasp on his metal lunch box, clicking it open and shut.

"Okay. I'll go, then. I'll make myself." Mina bit into the carrot.

Chapter Eleven

So on Saturday morning, Mina went to Ruth's house to practice the frog presentation.

It wasn't Ruth's turn to have the Friendship Ball, but Mina was taking no chances. She dropped it on the sofa, wondering if she'd ever see it again. Ruth might not want to pass the ball along anymore.

They set up the frog panel in Ruth's living room. First Ruth read, but so softly that Mina could barely hear her. As Mina read, her words felt like chunks of cold oatmeal in her mouth. The images of frogs Ruth pointed at with the long stick were faded and lifeless, printed with the old school printer.

After they'd gone through the presentation, Ruth made a pitcher of lemonade from a can. They carried the pitcher, two glasses, and a bag of chips outside to the table under the black walnut tree.

As Mina sat down in the lawn chair, she wished it was still the day the Fellow Friends had welcomed her into the group.

Little brown birds hopped along the branches of the walnut tree. Did they ever get jealous or scared?

She wanted to hide from Ruth, covering her face with the glass of lemonade. Instead, she said, "Ruth, do you think . . ." She paused, not knowing how to put it. "Do you think the Fellow Friends group is falling apart?"

Ruth looked up from her glass. "Why do you ask that?"

Mina shrugged and forced herself to go on. "Well, you and Sammy play alone a lot now. And Alana and I do, too."

"Yeah. I noticed." Ruth flicked a leaf off her forearm.

"This started when track started."

Ruth stared into her empty glass, as though studying the flecks of lemon pulp that clung to the sides.

Would she keep on staring into the glass, or set it down and leave? The conversation might end and never start up again. Mina thought of Sammy's idea. She was in a race. She had to keep talking. "I've never run before, at least not in races, or with anyone timing me," she said. "I didn't mean to tie you in the race. I didn't know I could."

"It wasn't your fault," Ruth said.

"But it still made you mad."

"Yeah. Sometimes."

Mina put down her glass and then picked it up again, needing something to hold on to. "But I didn't mean to tie you."

"Don't apologize."

A bird had landed on the other side of the table. It cocked its head, first to one side and then the other, eyeing the bag of chips. *Just one, please? Just a nibble?*

Ruth reached into the bag and tossed a chip toward the bird. It began to tug at it, trying to break off a bite. Two more flew down to help.

"You came out of nowhere and ran as fast as me," Ruth said. "I've worked all my life to be good at sports. I practice soccer three times a week. And here you come . . . But it's okay. Really, it's okay."

Mina felt like one of the tiny birds—out on the end of a branch, but with no wings. Yet she had to continue. "In the tryouts I tried to run slower."

"I know you did. And that was even worse. You know, Mina, when athletes compete, it isn't fair if someone doesn't try their hardest. You made me feel like I didn't really win. Or like at any time you could surprise me and beat me and I won't know what hit me."

"I didn't know what else to do."

"Yeah, I knew you lost on purpose because we're friends. A real athlete wouldn't have done that."

"But I'm not a real athlete," said Mina. "I'm a girlie girl."

Ruth laughed so loudly that the birds flew off. "You're one fast girlie girl."

Ruth's laughter made Mina laugh, too. Then she interlocked her fingers and looked down into the tight ball her hands made. She sighed and looked up. "I just want to be a Fellow Friend."

Ruth threw another chip to lure the birds back before turning to Mina. She squinted and screwed up her face against the bright sun. "It's too late. You're already more than a friend."

"What do you mean?"

"A friend is a friend. I've got lots. But there's not a lot of people I can race against." She paused. "I got an idea. I want to know something. Let's go over to the park right now and race."

Mina's legs suddenly felt as though they needed braces. She wondered if Wilma Rudolph had ever felt this weak. And yet there was no escaping this race.

"If you don't race, we'll never know if you can beat me. I'll never be able to think of myself as the fastest."

"Okay," Mina said slowly, thinking of Alana's secret. She had already beaten Ruth. "I'll race you."

Ruth held out her hands, the fingertips salty and greasy from the chips, ready for the Fellow Friends Handshake.

Chapter Twelve

The park was just down the street from Ruth's house. As they walked, Mina thought of how the Chinese Moon Festival was a special time to celebrate friendship. If only it were fall instead of spring. If only she could just offer Ruth a simple moon cake. . . .

When they reached the spread of green grass, Ruth headed for an olive tree with a patch of bare dirt underneath. "Let's run from that pine tree over there to here." She marked a line with her toe. "That's about fifty meters."

Mina nodded. Would it really be okay to win? She followed Ruth to the pine, where she marked a second line.

Ruth leaned into the tree trunk and stretched one leg behind her, bouncing into the heel.

Not wanting to copy Ruth, Mina bent over to touch her toes.

"Hey, guys," Ruth called to two small boys crossing the grass. She cupped her hands around her mouth: "Can you help us with our race?"

The boys came closer, one in a striped T-shirt, the other wearing a purple baseball cap turned backward.

Ruth beckoned to the one with the cap. "You stand here." She pointed to the start line she'd drawn. "You'll count down for us." She pointed to the line by the olive tree. "You're over there," she told the other boy. "Watch who puts their foot across the line first. Watch closely because the race could be close."

Mina suddenly wished Ruth would offer another Fellow Friends Handshake, but Ruth was busy wiping her palms on her shorts.

The boy counted—"Three, two, one"—and then shouted: "Go!"

Mina plunged forward, shoving hard against the dirt with her toes. All her holding back vanished. She was off!

But the next moment, as though a whisper of wind had crossed her path, she found herself slowing—like in the tryouts when she had fallen behind on purpose. Way behind. That had felt awful.

She'd won once. It was time to win again.

At that moment, the world fell silent. The air filled with the smell of orange blossoms, a thick haze of sweetness. The sunshine cascaded, lovely and soft, around her head and shoulders. The tiniest breeze lapped at her as she ran. There was all the time in the world to complete the short distance between here and the tree.

She didn't turn her head to look, but Mina knew that Ruth was running beside her. They ran like the African antelopes she'd seen in a movie—loping over a yellow plain, beneath trees with flat, horizontal branches.

One gigantic leap took Mina sailing high and forward, over the line. The leap carried her past the boy in the striped shirt.

The silence broke. "You won!" shouted the boy, pointing at Mina.

She glanced down at herself. Then, even though her breath was coming in great heaving gulps, she looked at Ruth.

Ruth was leaning over, her hands on her knees, breathing hard. Finally, she lifted her face and managed to smile.

The boys wandered off, and Mina and Ruth lay down on the grass, cradled in a large nest of miniature white flowers. Their breathing calmed into the same rhythm.

The sun was still up, but Mina noticed a crisp crescent in the sky. For the next two weeks it would grow until it reached its night of complete fullness. Mina closed her eyes. She was glad she'd run against Ruth. Like the moon, she was beginning to feel round and whole herself.

"Thanks," said Mina after the shadow of the olive tree had edged across their faces.

"For what?"

"For helping me try my best."

"If you don't run fast, you can't win," said Ruth.

"Or lose," said Mina.

"That's a funny thing to say."

"You know, I just realized that I copped out by getting into the relay," Mina said quietly.

"How do you mean?"

"I wanted to run fast but not risk anything."

"But if you run badly in the relay—like if you drop the baton—you blow it for everyone."

"That's what Coach said. But losing the race, even for all of us, even for the school, never seemed as bad as beating you and not being friends with you anymore."

Silently, Ruth began to pick the flowers that grew in the grass. "Here, a bouquet for the winner."

Mina reached out her thumb and forefinger to take the collection of tiny stems from her friend.

"Ruth," she said after the shadow of the olive tree had slipped over their hearts, "I've discovered a secret about myself."

"Hmm?"

"I love running. I love the way it feels. I love it more than anything."

"I know," Ruth said. "Me, too."

"There's the winning and losing part. And then there's the way it makes me happy."

"I forget that part," Ruth said quietly. "I just want to win."

Mina held Ruth's bouquet against the sky. The little daisies were so white, their centers so purple.

Chapter Thirteen

The Fellow Friends ate lunches together again,
gathering around the table to unwrap sandwiches
and pop open their plastic containers. Alana's
mom made a special bag for the Friendship Ball.
They wrote all their names on the bag with
permanent marker so the ball would never get
lost again.

Ruth announced a Fellow Friends party at her house, scheduled to take place after the meet even if the team lost.

A week after the City Meet, the whole class would be going to Ms. Jenner's house for a full-moon potluck dinner. Mina planned to take watermelon cut into the different shapes of the moon's phases.

"I'll be glad when this is over with and you can have fun again," said Alana.

In the early evenings, Mom and Mina jogged at the park. Poochie loved to run alongside them, yipping.

Paige was content on the swings. "Look, Mina!" she called out one evening.

Mina looked to see the moon appearing from behind the clouds.

"It's getting round like a winner's medal," Paige said.

Mina placed her hand over her chest where she hoped a medal would hang.

Mina finished *Seven Steps to Treasure.* In the end, Francesca got to keep all of the diamonds after the bad guy went to jail. Always cautious, Francesca placed the diamonds in a safety deposit box until her twenty-first birthday.

Mina handed the book to Mom. "Could you get me something more . . ."

"Challenging?" Mom offered.

"Yeah, I guess," Mina said.

All week she and the others ran the relay over and over in the afternoons until they glided through the routine, smoothly passing the baton. Sometimes Mina felt that instead of four separate girls, they'd become one creature that ran, passed, ran, passed, and ran again.

If they won, they would be going to City. If they won at City, they would stand on a podium while the high-school band played the National Anthem, just like in the Olympics. Sometimes Mina whispered, "City" to herself just before she went to sleep.

By the end of the week, the light side of the moon was winning over the dark. As Mina drew it, she thought of the fact that no matter how many times the moon disappeared, it always grew back. Someday she might run against Ruth again and lose. Or lose against another girl. But like the moon, if she lost, she would also win again.

On the day of the track meet, Mina paused at the entry of Duncan Berring Elementary School. The playground was a solid mass of kids from the four schools, everyone practicing their running and jumping and throwing. A hot little breeze whipped the bunches of balloons and flags marking the events. It fluttered the school banners. Shouts, laughter, and the sound of the coaches' whistles blended into a roar.

Mina saw Alana threading her way through the crowd.

"There you are," Alana called out. "I have something for you." She handed Mina a four-leaf clover. "It took me a whole hour to find it."

Mina twirled the stem between her thumb and forefinger. "Thanks, Alana. This feels lucky. Do you think we'll win?"

Alana shrugged. "There's nothing stopping you."

When it was time for the race, Mina's heart beat like the wings of the butterfly that Sammy had once brought to school in a jar. The heat of the black track passed through the soles of her shoes. The moment had come. Very soon it would be over.

It took a few minutes to get the four teams placed along the oval of the track.

"Why aren't we all lined up evenly?" Mina asked Coach.

"We stagger you because the lanes are not

the same length—the inside is shortest, the outside longest. We're arranging you like this to make the race fair."

The pistol shot broke the air into pieces and the first four girls took off.

Mina looked across the track, trying to see which of the four girls would hand over the baton first. *Run, run, run,* she chanted in her head.

It was Cassie!

Liz dove ahead, the baton gleaming in the sunlight.

Mina stretched her arm behind her, her whole body reaching with the effort to get the magic wand of the baton. When Liz was about to arrive, Mina began to jog forward until Liz caught up with her. Mina felt the baton land in her hand, slippery and heavy and important.

Liz let go and Mina took off at full speed. The cheers of the crowd launched her like exploding firecrackers.

She was a Moon Runner flying to the moon.

Flying to harvest the fruit of the Moon Tree. Hurling forward, she could almost taste the sweetness.

Ruth began to jog as Mina drew near. Mina hurled herself forward one last time and delivered the baton to Ruth.

When Mina turned, Ruth was gone, leaping toward the finish line. A whistle blew, and then Ruth was holding her arms in the air, joining hands with Liz. And Cassie lifted Mina's arm and they ran together to join the others.

All four were screaming and shouting. Mina found her throat filled with happy cries. Their relay team had won!

Mina looked up into the bleachers. She found Alana and her family, Mom and Daddy and Paige, standing together cheering. Alana held up her fingers in a V for *Victory*. Paige was waving as she bobbed up and down.

Mina felt Coach's big hand pat her back in congratulations. "You'll be going to City now."

Mina's head spun with joy.

She, Liz, Cassie, and Ruth hugged in a tight circle of four. As Mina laughed and babbled with the others, she sensed circles extending beyond the relay team—her family, Sammy and Alana, the round globe of the earth itself, filled with springtime, and beyond even that, the moon, growing and dying and growing each month in the sky.

ACKNOWLEDGMENTS

I would like to acknowledge the members of the Hive who encouraged me in the first draft of this story: Gretchen Woelfle, Mary Ann Downing, JoAnn Macken, Phyllis Harris, April Sayre, Jeanne Marie Grunwell, Meribeth Shanks, and Laura Kemp; Irma Shephard for her intuitive reading; Ann Collins for her eagle eye edits; and my editors, Deborah Wayshak and Amy Erhlich, who, as always, led me to the heart of the story.

READ CAROLYN MARSDEN'S LATEST NOVEL

When Heaven Fell

Hardcover ISBN 978-0-7636-3175-8

Turn the page for an excerpt. . . .

Chapter One

Binh's fruit stand was sheltered by corrugated tin on three sides and by a large umbrella overhead. The canvas of the umbrella had rotted away long ago.

"Mr. Thang! Come for your soda!" Binh called.

Old Mr. Thang crossed the street.

"My pleasure, Granduncle," said Binh, handing over the can of Orange Crush.

Although Mr. Thang hadn't paid cash for the drink, later he would bring a load of charcoal to the house.

Trucks and motorcycles passed back and forth on the highway, four lanes of black asphalt. Gray exhaust

An excerpt from *When Heaven Fell*

colored the concrete buildings, the speeding vehicles, and even the face of Mrs. Tran across the highway, selling her flat baskets of bok choy and ginger.

Every vehicle honked—either a series of quick beeps or a steady blast.

Binh took off the cotton mask she wore for protection against the fumes. She wiped her forehead with it. The day had been long and hot.

Binh's cousin Cuc rode up on her old bicycle, wearing a dress with red flowers. Cuc was a year older than Binh and half a head taller. Her black hair was cut in a short bowl, while Binh's fell to her shoulders.

"Did I get bicycle grease on my dress, Binh?" Cuc lifted the fabric to examine the hem.

"I don't see any. Or maybe just a little spot right there . . ."

Cuc gave Binh the clothes she outgrew. Binh couldn't wait until the pretty red dress—now dirtied with a dab of oil—would be hers.

Cuc not only had the red dress and a bicycle, but often wore colorful bracelets from her mother's tourist

An excerpt from *When Heaven Fell*

shop. The shop made enough that Third Aunt, unlike Binh's mother, wasn't always complaining about money.

Just then, three boys and two girls came down the highway in their blue and white elementary-school uniforms — white shirts with round collars, dark blue pants for the boys, skirts for the girls. Each carried an armload of books.

The boys went on while the girls stopped by the stand.

Binh pulled her cone-shaped hat low over her face.

"How much are the fruit cups?" one girl asked.

"A thousand *dong,*" Binh answered, studying the ground.

As each girl handed over a bill and helped herself to the yellow fruit, Binh kept her hat pulled down.

Watching the girls catch up with the boys, Cuc said, "They think they're better than us!"

Binh jumped up and imitated the girls' walk — stiff-legged, nose in the air. Then she picked up a small pebble and tossed it after them.

An excerpt from *When Heaven Fell*

Cuc laughed, the streamers on her handlebars jiggling. Yet in spite of the way they poked fun at the schoolchildren, whenever those children came close, both Binh and Cuc lowered their eyes.

Instead of going to school, Binh worked at the fruit stand and Cuc helped her mother in the tourist shop.

Binh had heard that at school one learned not only about America, but about other places as well. School sounded like a huge doorway to the world, a doorway through which Binh longed to walk.

But Binh didn't like to think about school since her family couldn't afford to send her. School was for the sons and daughters of families who had large businesses in town and for paid members of the Communist Party. School wasn't for her.

"Let me have that last cup of fruit," Cuc demanded.

Binh shook her head.

"Please. Look. It has flies on it. You can't sell that."

"I *will* sell it." Binh slapped at Cuc's reaching hand.

An excerpt from *When Heaven Fell*

Across the highway, two high-school girls bicycled past, the tunics and loose trousers of their white *ao dai* fluttering.

Cuc gazed after them. Neither she nor Binh mocked the older girls.

Binh turned to the box tied to Cuc's bicycle. "What's in that package?"

"Paper fans. The bus dropped them off this morning."

"Are they pretty?" Binh asked.

Cuc shrugged. "I haven't opened them yet. But Ma is eager to sell them. I'd better get going." She pedaled off, her bicycle entering the throng of motorcycles and small cars on the highway.

An excerpt from *When Heaven Fell*

AND ALSO BY CAROLYN MARSDEN

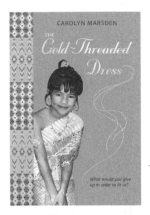

Hardcover
ISBN 978-0-7636-1569-7

Paperback
ISBN 978-0-7636-2993-9

Hardcover
ISBN 978-0-7636-2635-8

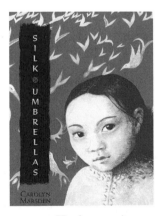

Hardcover
ISBN 978-0-7636-2257-2

*Co-written with
Virginia Shin-Mui Loh*

Hardcover
ISBN 978-0-7636-3012-6